CHANGE MAKERS

12 POLITICAL LEADERS WHO CHANGED THE WORLD

BLACK RABBIT BOOKS

MATTHEW McCABE

Table of Contents

Alexander the Great was a successful ruler and military leader.

Alexander the Great Expands *World Views*

1

Alexander the Great led the Kingdom of Macedonia in 336 BCE. The kingdom was part of Ancient Greece. Alexander had great military victories.

During this time, people rarely traveled. They did not usually leave their town or kingdom. They did not know much about the rest of the world. Alexander brought Greek culture to them.

Alexander was a talented military leader. He thought up new ways to beat stronger forces. His troops were split into groups. Soldiers stood shoulder-to-shoulder in long rows. This kept enemies away. Fighters on horseback were called **cavalry**. They helped win against strong forces. Alexander led his army against the Persian **Empire**. He never lost a battle.

Alexander and his army traveled for eight years. They covered more than 11,000 miles (17,703 kilometers). Alexander **founded** 70 cities. His empire grew. It crossed Europe, Asia, and Africa. He opened trade routes between India and Europe. Spices, cloth, and luxury items were traded across the continents.

Greek language and culture brought the empire together. Alexander learned about other **customs** and languages too. This helped him become a better ruler.

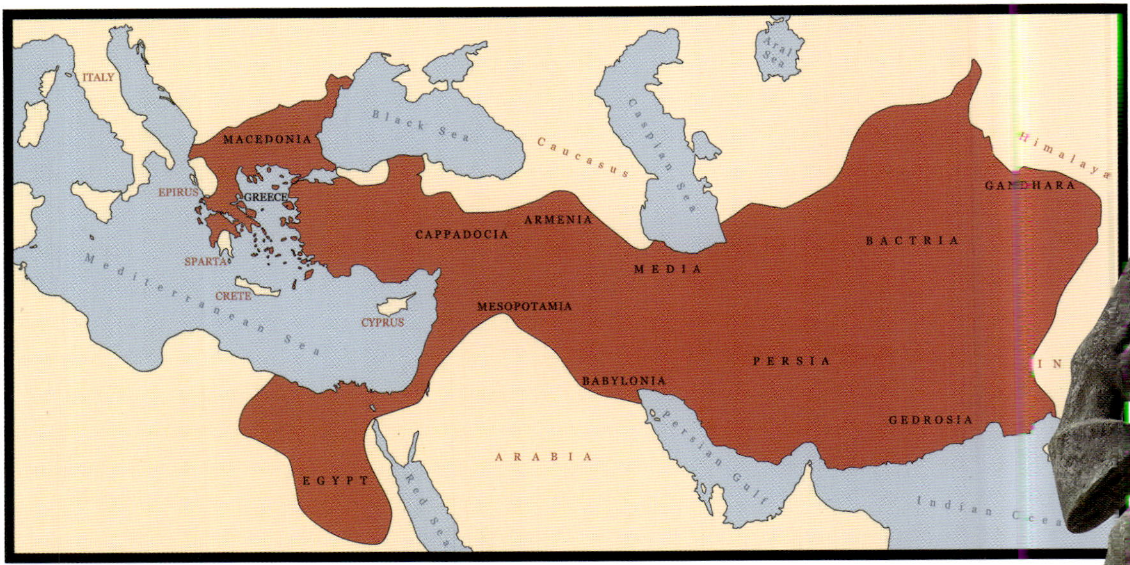

Alexander's empire covered three continents.

2 million Number of square miles (5.18 million sq km) that Alexander's empire covered.

Alexander spread Greek language and culture around the world. • He started the first trade routes between different regions of the world. • He learned foreign ways to help him rule.

Susan B. Anthony Leads *US Women Forward*

2

Before 1920, only white men could vote in the United States. However, many women wanted to change that. They worked hard to do so. Susan B. Anthony was one of these women. Anthony was born in 1820. She believed all people were equal. This helped guide her later in life. She fought for women to have a greater voice in American society.

US Silver Dollar coin featuring Susan B. Anthony.

Anthony's family fought to end enslavement. Her father stood against it. Young Anthony listened to anti-slavery speeches. She went to meetings. Her passion for the cause grew. Soon, she began giving her own speeches. People came to meetings she planned. It was her time to speak up for women.

Women had fewer rights during Anthony's lifetime. Men were in charge. They passed laws that worked best for them. Women's thoughts were not taken seriously.

14 Years between Anthony's death and passage of the 19th Amendment.

Anthony fought for women's right to vote in the United States. • She led suffrage associations. As a leader, she toured the country to gain more support. • Anthony fought for equal pay for women. She wanted women to be able to vote.

In the 1870s, Anthony fought for women's suffrage. Suffrage is the right to vote. Anthony traveled the country. She spoke to many people about women's rights.

Anthony's biggest act was in 1872. She voted during the presidential election. It was against the law for a woman to vote. Police arrested her. She was also fined $100. That is more than $2,000 today. However, she never paid the fine.

Anthony helped found a group in 1877. It was called the National American Woman Suffrage Association. She helped lead the suffrage movement until her death. In 1906, Anthony passed away. The 19th Amendment was passed in 1920. It gave women the right to vote. Some people called it the Susan B. Anthony Amendment.

Women demand to be able to vote in Yonkers, New York, in 1913.

ANTHONY'S OTHER CAUSES Anthony's efforts gave women a voice. Yet she fought for many other causes too. Equal pay for female teachers was one of them. Supporting women who worked in printing was another. Anthony also wanted women to have the right to own property.

Sirimavo Bandaranaike Leads *Sri Lanka*

3

Sirimavo Bandaranaike was elected **prime minister** of Sri Lanka in 1960. Her election changed the world. Before, no woman had ever held this office.

Sri Lanka had been ruled by the United Kingdom. It won its independence in 1948. Bandaranaike's husband was elected prime minister in 1956. He was killed in 1959. His political party needed a new leader. Bandaranaike was chosen to lead. She won the election a year later. She became prime minister.

Bandaranaike made a lot of changes. She changed the country's national language. It used to be English. She changed it to Sinhalese. That was the language of the island's largest ethnic group. People were given chances for better education. Students could now learn about native culture. They could learn about

Bandaranaike at work after winning the election for prime minister in 1960.

native **heritage**. These became school subjects. However, some people thought the changes would come at a cost.

The prime minister's work divided the people in the country. The Sinhalese people made up most of Sri Lanka. Changes worked in their favor. The Tamils were another group of people. They often suffered.

Bandaranaike stood up for Sri Lanka when she talked with other world leaders. Many of those leaders were men. She made them listen. Through change, she showed the world that a woman could run a modern country.

Think About It World leaders make a lot of decisions. Sometimes people disagree with them. Think of a rule or law you disagree with. Write a paragraph telling why you disagree. Use examples to back up your opinion.

18 Number of years Bandaranaike served as prime minister of Sri Lanka.

Bandaranaike led the country after it won independence. • She gave Sri Lankans more chances for education. • She showed the world women could lead a modern country.

Bandaranaike helped more children get an education.

Winston Churchill Calls *for Aid*

4

Winston Churchill was the prime minister of the United Kingdom (UK). In the early years of World War II (1939–45), the UK fought against Germany. The Germans had already defeated France. The UK needed a strong leader. Churchill was elected in 1940. His first action was to unify the British people. He gave speeches that told people to be brave. Churchill wanted to win the war.

By 1940, Germany's army had moved further into Europe. Some of the areas had British troops fighting there. But it seemed nothing could stop Germany. Its next step would be to invade the UK.

The UK had fewer troops and supplies than Germany. But Churchill still wanted the country to fight hard. The Battle of Britain took place in September 1940.

Churchill's toughness helped him lead the United Kingdom during World War II.

4 Number of volumes in Churchill's memoir of World War II.

Churchill's determination helped the United Kingdom stand against Germany. • He believed the UK could win the war. • He enlisted the help of the United States and the Soviet Union.

The German military bombed the UK. But they weren't able to take over.

Churchill was determined. It helped him gain support. British fighters got tanks, planes, and bullets from ally countries. Churchill met with US President Franklin D. Roosevelt. He also talked with Soviet Premier Joseph Stalin. They worked together. United, they beat Germany in World War II.

Churchill makes a speech in 1946 after the end of World War II.

MAN OF THE PEOPLE Churchill was a man of the people. His speeches about the war effort made a big impact. The way he looked also helped. Churchill had been in the military and was leading a country at war. Instead of a uniform though, he became known for his stylish suits. His non-military dress helped reassure the British people.

Shirin Ebadi Provides *a Voice for Women*

5

Shirin Ebadi lives in Iran. As a lawyer, she fights for the rights of women and children. There have been many challenges to overcome. However, her career has been one of many successes. Many of the things she has done are unthinkable for a woman in her country.

Ebadi was chosen as a city court judge in 1969. She worked in the capital city of Tehran. She was the first female judge in Iran. Five years later, she became the president of the city court. In 1979, she met her first big challenge.

Iran went through an Islamic **Revolution**. Life in the nation was forever changed. It got rid of the monarch. A new Islamic republic was created. The new leaders did not treat women the same way as men. Ebadi was not allowed to be a judge. The new leaders did not want women in power.

Finally, Ebadi was able to practice law again in 1992. She became a lawyer. She took cases that challenged the government. She fought for the right to speak against things the government did. Her main focus was on the rights of women and children. They still do not have many rights in Iran.

Ebadi founded two organizations. They both support Iranians in court. She was honored with a Nobel Peace Prize in 2003. She was the first female Muslim and first Iranian to win the award. In 2009, she was exiled from Iran. She cannot enter her home country anymore. But she still fights for Iranian children and women.

Iranians wave flags and banners to protest unjust laws.

DEFENDER OF WOMEN AND CHILDREN Ebadi had a case that fought to change custody laws. A young Iranian girl could not live with her mother after a divorce. The law usually sided with fathers. A girl once died in the care of her father and stepmother. Ebadi was the mother's lawyer. She helped change the law. It gives mothers a better chance of getting their children back.

3 Number of weeks Ebadi spent in jail in 2000 during one of her human rights cases.

Ebadi is a pioneer of women's rights in Iran. • She fights for children's rights in Iran and around the globe. • She was exiled from Iran in 2009 but still fights for equal rights.

Ebadi fights for human rights in Iran.

Ebadi's work has helped other Iranians stand up for human rights

Queen Elizabeth Inspires *a Kingdom*

6

Queen Elizabeth I ruled England from 1558 to 1603. She showed the world that women could lead nations. Her father was King Henry VIII. All her siblings had died. She was next in line for the throne. Some people did not think a woman should lead. They tried to replace her with men. Others tried to put a woman controlled by men in charge. Elizabeth did not back down.

Elizabeth was not like other leaders. She never married. Some historians think she did not want a king to take her power. She was smart. She spoke six languages. Elizabeth saw herself as a capable leader. This leadership helped unite England.

King Henry VIII

Protestants and Catholics were in a battle to control the government. Elizabeth was a Protestant. People of her religion had control of the country. Elizabeth did not treat people from other religions badly, though. She allowed some Catholic traditions to keep going.

Elizabeth helped create a Golden Age for England. Trade with other countries grew a lot. Arts and culture did well during this time too. Artists and writers created great works for Elizabeth.

The English people supported Queen Elizabeth I during her reign.

COMMANDER ELIZABETH Elizabeth was also a great military leader. The Spanish were trying to invade the country. The Spanish wanted a Catholic ruler in England. British forces were getting ready to fight. Elizabeth visited the battlefield. She gave a speech. It inspired the English troops. They went on to defeat the Spanish.

Elizabeth I proved a queen could lead a nation.

44 Number of years Elizabeth I was Queen of England.

Some historians believe that Elizabeth did not want a king to rule England. • She united the English Protestants and Catholics. • During her reign, trade and the arts flourished.

7 Mahatma Gandhi Fights *Government Abuse*

Mahatma Gandhi was born in 1869. India was a British colony at the time. Gandhi was a small, quiet man. However, he had a big vision. After a long fight, his work helped India gain independence.

Gandhi believed in fighting without violence. He thought this would embarrass the British rulers. **Poverty** and hunger were big problems in India. Gandhi believed that giving people control over their futures would help. In the 1920s, he led efforts to build new schools and hospitals. He wanted his people to have access to education, good health, and equal rights. But British rulers arrested him for causing trouble.

In the 1930s, Gandhi inspired people. He asked them to only buy goods that were made in their

Gandhi worked to improve the lives of Indian people and gain independence for India.

country. They should not be giving their money to the British. The British did not let Indian companies make and sell salt. Instead, the people had to pay a high tax to buy it. Gandhi led a march in **protest** in 1930.

The march went from Gandhi's home to the coast. Many people followed him. They marched for more than 240 miles (386 km). Gandhi and thousands of his supporters were arrested. The world noticed Gandhi's efforts. It also saw how poorly the British treated Indian people. Gandhi believed this would help India gain its freedom. Finally, in 1947, India became independent.

WORLDWIDE IMPACT Gandhi's beliefs inspired American civil rights leaders. Martin Luther King Jr. used Gandhi's teachings to develop a plan for protesting without violence. These protests would help end segregation in America.

Gandhi leads protesters on the march to the coast in 1930.

60,000 Estimated number of people arrested during Gandhi's march to the coast.

Gandhi worked to help India gain its freedom from British rule. • He led a march protesting poor British treatment. • He influenced civil rights leaders in the United States.

Martin Luther King Jr. Works to Advance *Civil Rights*

8

Slavery ended in the United States after the US Civil War (1861–65). However, Black people were still not treated equally. Racism continued into the 1950s. Dr. Martin Luther King Jr. wanted Black people to have equal rights. He led the movement to help them get it.

The southern United States was segregated. Black children had to go to different schools than white children. Black people had to sit in different sections in public places. They also faced racism at work. King Jr. wanted to change this.

Black and white people rode public buses. During this time, Black people were forced to give up their seats to white people. They had to sit or stand in the back. In 1955, King Jr. led the Montgomery bus **boycott**. Many Black people refused to use the city's buses. They

King Jr. spoke about segregation at a press conference.

381 Number of days the Montgomery bus boycott lasted.

- King Jr. fought to end segregation in the South.
- He taught people to protest without using violence.
- He worked for full voting rights for Black voters.

protested unfair treatment. This cost the bus system a lot of money. The segregated bus rules were dropped. King Jr. and his supporters had won their first battle.

King Jr. planned more protests. They called attention to inequality. The protesters stayed peaceful. They were often met with violence in return. Protesters were attacked with police dogs and water hoses. The country finally did something in 1964. Congress passed the Civil Rights Act. This made it illegal to deny work and services because of someone's race.

King Jr. worked to make it easier for Black people to vote.

THE RIGHT TO VOTE The Voting Rights Act of 1965 made it easier for Black people to vote. Before it was passed, some towns and states made Black voters pass a test. Others made them pay a tax. The Voting Rights Act banned these things. King Jr. worked to get the act passed.

Abraham Lincoln Preserves *the Union*

9

Abraham Lincoln was president of the United States. He was elected in 1860. The nation was in trouble. In the South, people were enslaved. Southern leaders did not want that to change. In the North, enslaving people was not allowed. Northerners wanted the practice to end. Lincoln was one of these people.

Human enslavement had existed since the nation began. It was a big issue. Lincoln saw that the country was divided. The North was called the Union. The Southern states left the US to make their own nation. It was called the Confederacy. The two nations fought in the US Civil War. Lincoln's goal was to preserve the nation. He led the Union army. They won. In 1863, Lincoln signed the Emancipation Proclamation. It freed all enslaved people in the country.

Lincoln guided the Union and freed Southern enslaved people during his presidency.

11 Number of states where enslaved people were freed by the Emancipation Proclamation.

Lincoln helped the Union with smart leadership during the Civil War. • He ended slavery in the southern United States. • He supported laws that helped the United States expand westward.

Lincoln helped the country grow. The Homestead Act gave people the chance to move across the country. If they built a home, they could earn 160 acres (65 hectares) of land. Lincoln also passed the Morrill Act. It started public universities in every state. He laid the foundation for the United States to keep growing.

The Homestead Act helped people move to states like Wyoming.

Think About It Lincoln expanded the power of the president during the Civil War. This "war power" let him do things without getting permission from Congress and the courts. He did this so the Union could win the war. Should the president be able to ignore Congress during war? Why or why not?

Lincoln speaks to Union officers on the battlefield at Antietam, Maryland, in 1862.

Nelson Mandela Stops *Apartheid*

10

White leaders had controlled South Africa for decades. But most of the people who lived there were Black. Many of them lived in poverty. They were suffering from apartheid. This was a system of racial segregation. Black people had to live separately from white people. Black people had to go to separate schools. People of different races could not work together.

Nelson Mandela helped bring equality and **democracy** to the people of his country. Mandela was a leader in the fight against apartheid. Because of his work, he spent 27 years in jail. In 1990, he was finally released. Mandela rejoined the fight right away. He worked with the president of the country. They both knew things needed to change. Together, they came up with basic freedoms and political rights for all South Africans.

Mandela fought for equal rights for Black South Africans.

27 Number of years Mandela spent in prison for trying to end apartheid.

Mandela fought for equal justice and freedoms in South Africa. • With the president of South Africa, Mandela ended apartheid. • He was the country's first Black leader.

Mandela was elected president of South Africa in 1994. He was the country's first Black leader. With his help, the country began to heal. Yet, he was more than a politician. He also fought for equal rights. Giving back to the people was important. He started foundations to help the nation. The Nelson Mandela Children's Fund helps change how society treats young children.

Mandela shares the stage with South Africa's President F. W. de Klerk (left).

46664 46664 is a concert series. It is named after Mandela's prison number. The concerts are performed all over the world. They raise money to support HIV/AIDS research in Africa. HIV/AIDS is a big problem in Africa. In 2018, 25.7 million people in Africa were living with the disease. That same year, 470,000 died from it.

Franklin D. Roosevelt Leads *a Nation*

11

Franklin D. Roosevelt was elected US president in 1932. This was during the Great Depression. Many people did not have jobs. Those who did were making less money than they used to. The country was struggling.

Roosevelt came up with new policies and programs. They were called the New Deal. The programs gave the government new roles and power. He also made new services. Social Security was one of them. The program gives financial support to elderly and disabled Americans.

In 1939, World War II began in Europe. The American people wanted to stay out of the war. Roosevelt listened to them. He did not ignore what was happening across the ocean, though. Instead, Roosevelt helped Britain and its allies against Germany. US tanks, planes, guns, and bullets were shipped to Europe.

Roosevelt led the United States through financial trouble and World War II.

This policy changed on December 7, 1941. That day, Japan attacked Pearl Harbor, Hawaii. This was a US Navy base. The attack changed how people felt about the war. The country now supported sending troops. Roosevelt spoke to Congress. He asked them to declare war. They did and America joined the war.

Radio was a new technology at the time. Roosevelt used it to talk to the public. His conversations felt personal, not like a speech. The talks were known as fireside chats. They helped people trust what he was doing for the country.

The Civilian Conservation Corps was a New Deal program. It put young men to work on public projects.

Think About It Roosevelt is the only US president to serve four terms. Before 1951, there was no limit on how many times a president could be elected into office. Most stopped after two terms. But Roosevelt believed it was better if the president did not change during hard times. He thought it was better for the country to have a steady leader. Many questioned his decision. Do you think it was wrong to keep leading? Why or why not?

12.8 million Number of Americans out of work when Roosevelt took office.

Roosevelt led the United States during World War II. • He created new policies to lift America out of financial trouble. • His new policies gave the government new rules and powers.

12 George Washington Champions *Democracy*

George Washington shaped the United States from the start. He led the Continental Army during the American Revolution (1775–83). There were 13 colonies. They fought for independence from England. Washington was a smart leader. He kept soldiers on the battlefield. He got other leaders to support the cause. The country won its independence.

Washington was more than a war hero. He wanted to go back to a normal life after the war. However, people wanted him to lead the new country. A group of people helped him run the new country. Some of them helped write the US Constitution. What they wrote formed the US government.

Washington was given the chance to be a king in America. However, he did not want the new country

George Washington helped win the Revolutionary War. He shaped the new United States.

to have a king. Washington thought people should elect their leaders. So the people voted. They elected Washington the first president. He served two four-year terms. He decided not to run again in 1796. Most future presidents followed his example.

Washington helped build a new nation. The citizens got to choose their leaders. He made choices that still affect the country today. He supported national taxes. The national bank was another thing he supported. It loans people and the government money.

A painting shows Washington leading troops at Valley Forge, Pennsylvania.

WASHINGTON THE SLAVEHOLDER Washington was not a perfect man. Many white American men enslaved people at that time. Washington was one of them. He held 317 enslaved people. He never freed them during his life. In his will, he said that all his enslaved people should be freed after his wife's death.

8 Number of years Washington led the Continental Army.

Washington was the first US president. • Future presidents were shaped by his actions. • He believed in freedom of the people.

How You Can Make a Change

Protest Peacefully

Many political leaders found success without using violence. Look around your neighborhood or school. If you find something that needs improving, take action. Write a polite letter to your mayor or principal. Ask friends and family members to sign the letter.

Sign a Petition

Petitions are written requests for change. To show their support, many people may sign a single petition. Is there something you would like to change at school or in your neighborhood? If so, write a petition. Ask for your principal or local government to make the change. With the help of an adult, gather as many signatures as you can. This shows your idea is supported by the community.

Write to Your Representative or Senator

Is there a state or national law you would like to change? Even though kids cannot vote, they can write to be heard. They can send letters to their representatives and senators in the state capitol or Washington, D.C. Write a polite letter stating your opinion. Be sure to include lots of reasons why you believe what you do.

Glossary

boycott
Refuse to buy, use, or participate in activities as a way of protesting.

cavalry
Soldiers who fight on horseback.

custom
An action or way of behaving that is usual and traditional among the people in a particular place.

democracy
A form of government in which people vote for leaders.

empire
A group of countries or regions that are controlled by one ruler or one government.

found
To begin or create.

heritage
The traditions, achievements, and beliefs that are part of the history of a group or nation.

poverty
The state of being poor.

prime minister
The head of the government in some countries.

protest
To say or do something that shows disagreement.

segregation
The practice of keeping people of different races separate.

For More Information

Books

Forbes, Megan DuVarney. *Leaders and Thinkers in American History: 15 Influential People You Should Know.* Emeryville, CA: Rockridge Press, 2021.

Jazynka, Kitson. *Susan B. Anthony.* Washington, DC: National Geographic Kids, 2019.

Murray, Laura K. *Mahatma Gandhi.* Mankato, MN: Creative Education, 2019.

Websites

BBC: Queen Elizabeth I
www.bbc.co.uk/bitesize/topics/zkrkscw/articles/zkh7bdm

National Geographic Kids: Martin Luther King Jr.
www.kids.nationalgeographic.com/explore/history/martin-luther-king-jr

 • Top Rank is an imprint of Black Rabbit Books. • Edited by Book Buddy Media • Designed by Danny Nanos • Photographs © Alamy: Keren Su/China Span, 12; AP: Associated Press, 16, Jerome Delay, 35, Sipa, 17; Dreamstime: Mirko Kuzmanovic, 24-25, Spiroview Inc., 21; Getty: Bettmann, 11, 26, ChrisHepburn, 18, Flip Schulke Archives, 23, Hulton Archive, 22, Hulton Deutsch, 24–25, 44; Library of Congress: 8, 10, 15, 21, Alexander Gardner, 33, Anthony Berger, 30–31, 45, Bain News Service, 9, 44, Carol M. Highsmith, 36, Elias Goldensky, 37, Gilbert Stuart, 41, Leffler, Warren K., 29, Mydans, Carl, 38, Percy Moran, 42; Peter Hermes Furian, 6; Shutterstock: Anastasios71, 7, BOOCYS, 2–3, Charles HB Mercer, [illegible], Christian Bertrand, 2–3, David Smart, 40, Everett Collection, 23, 30–31, 39, Frank L Junior, 8, John Cairns, 14, Kamira, [illegible]–5, Kiwi Innovation, cover, 43, lazyllama, 27, Lefteris Papaulakis, 32, nyker, 32, Phil Pasquini, 20, Rihardzz, 19, Ververidis Vasilis, 4–5, VladyslaV Travel photo, 13, wantanddo, 38 • Printed in China.

Library of Congress Cataloging-in-Publication Data: Names: Mccabe, Matthew, author. Title: 12 political leaders who changed the world / Matthew McCabe. Description: Mankato, MN : Black Rabbit Books, [2025] | Series: Change makers | Includes bibliographical references and index. | Audience: Ages 8–13 | Audience: Grades 4–6 | Identifiers: LCCN 2023052897 (print) | LCCN 2023052898 (ebook) | ISBN 9781645822943 (hardcover) | ISBN 9781645823261 (paperback) | ISBN 9781645823582 (ebook) | Subjects: LCSH: Heads of state—Biography—Juvenile literature. | Political activists—Biography—Juvenile literature. Classification: LCC D412 .M43 2025 (print) | LCC D412 (ebook) | DDC 920.009–dc23/eng/20231122

Index

About the Author

Matthew McCabe is a freelance writer and copywriter. He lives in Plymouth, Minnesota, raising his daughter and dog when he is not writing. He has worked as a writer for six years, covering a variety of topics ranging from business and travel to political leaders.